Raggedy Ann & Andy's

W9-BUU-618

THE PLAY IN THE ATTIC

A LYNX BOOK

This book is published by Lynx Books, a division of Lynx Communications, Inc., 41 Madison Avenue, New York, New York 10010. The name "Lynx" together with the logotype consisting of a stylized head of a lynx is a trademark of Lynx Communications, Inc.

Raggedy Ann and Andy's Grow-and-Learn Library, the names and depictions of Raggedy Ann, Raggedy Andy and all related characters are trademarks of Macmillan, Inc.

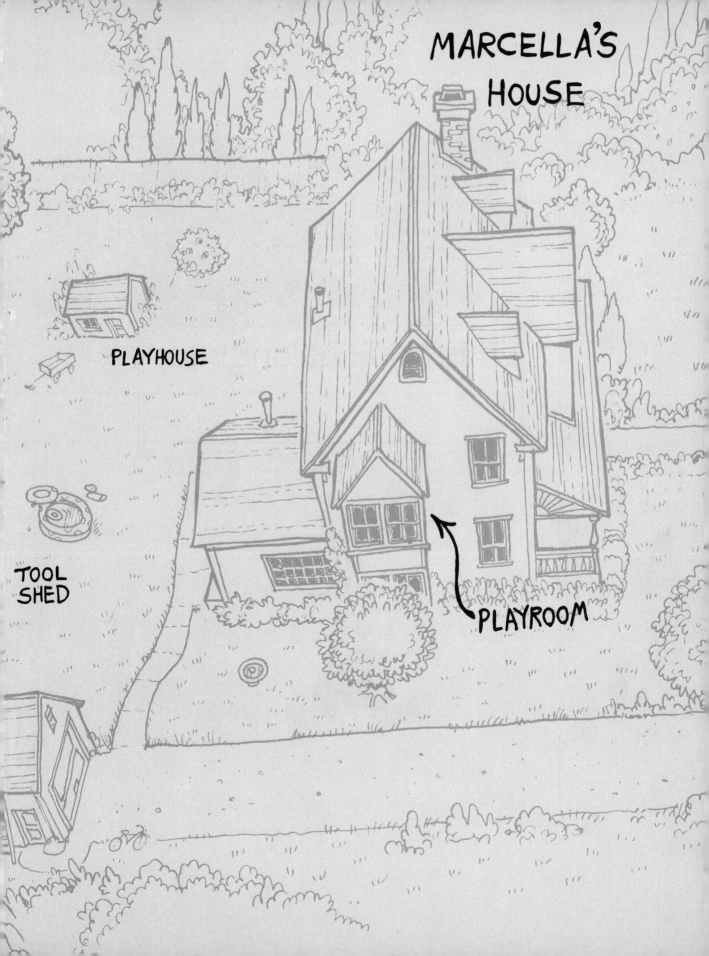

MARCELLA'S
HOUSE

PLAYHOUSE

PLAYROOM

TOOL
SHED

This book belongs to:

Raggedy Andy was looking forward to nighttime when Marcella and her family went to bed. He was thinking about the pillow fight he was going to start. He grinned to himself as he pictured the scene. It would be so much fun to take the other dolls by surprise!

Raggedy Cat was daydreaming, too. Last night she had discovered her own way of playing checkers. Tonight she would bat the rest of the pieces across the floor.

Tim the Toy Soldier and Percy the Policeman Doll didn't know about Raggedy Cat's plans. They were hoping to play checkers, too, if only they could find the pieces that had gotten misplaced.

Babette the French Doll was looking forward to playing "fairy princess" in the beautiful new gown that Marcella's mother had bought for her.

As the dolls sat thinking about their late-night plans, Marcella came into the playroom.

"I'm afraid I have to pack you all up for a couple of days," she said. "The painters are coming to work all over the house. I'll put you in the attic so that you don't get in the way."

"Painters!" thought Raggedy Andy with a terrible sinking feeling. "Attic!" So much for his pillow-fight idea.

"Painters!" thought the other dolls. Memories of the last time the painters came flashed through their heads. Things hadn't returned to normal for weeks!

"I guess there won't be any bedtime stories tonight," sighed The Camel with the Wrinkled Knees.

After Marcella's family had gone to bed, the playroom dolls began to look around the attic.

Grouchy Bear was starting to feel grouchier than ever. "Nobody asked us if we wanted the playroom painted," he grumbled.

"I was going to practice my magic tricks," wailed Bubbles the Clown Doll. "I wonder where they put my top hat."

"It's probably packed away with *my* lovely new gown," sighed Babette.

"All our plans are ruined!" cried Raggedy Andy, throwing up his hands.

Raggedy Ann looked around the attic. "Sometimes things don't work out the way we've planned," she said thoughtfully. "But we should just try to make the best of it. I could tell you a story from one of Marcella's storybooks," she suggested. "I remember most of them by heart."

"But I like to see the pictures," Sunny Bunny complained.

"Maybe we could act out the stories," suggested Raggedy Andy.

"That's a great idea!" Raggedy Ann agreed. "We could put on a play!"

"But what can we use for a stage and curtains?" asked Babette.

"There are some old curtains in one of the trunks," said Sunny Bunny. Sunny Bunny had spent many years living in the attic, so he knew just where to find everything.

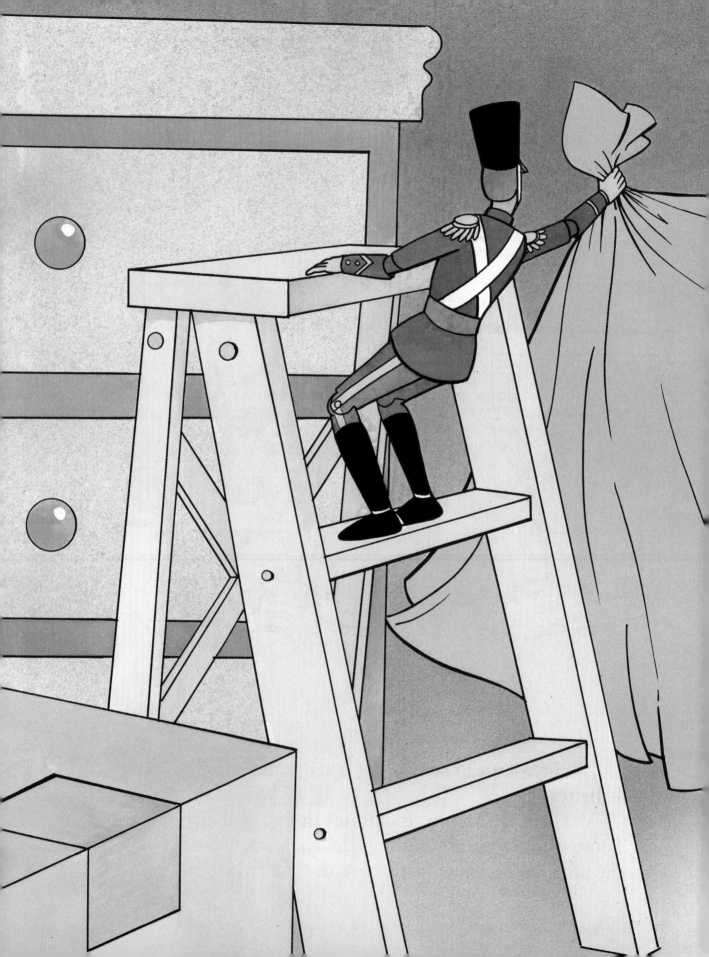

"I can hold up this side of the curtain," offered Tim as he set up a stepladder. Percy climbed on top of a trunk and volunteered to hold up the other side.

"I'll be the light man," said Sunny Bunny, running over to a big box and taking out a flashlight.

"But what story shall we act out?" asked Greta the Dutch Doll.

" 'Goldilocks and the Three Bears' is one of my favorites," said Babette.

"Yeah!" shouted Grouchy Bear. "That's a great story."

Raggedy Ann laughed. "I think I know who could play the parts of Goldilocks and Baby Bear," she said. "And we've read that story so many times that we won't even have to practice our parts!"

"Good," said Raggedy Ann. "Now we just need a storyteller. That's the person who tells what is going on when no one else is speaking."

"You know all the stories the best," The Camel told her. Everyone agreed that Raggedy Ann would be the perfect storyteller.

Babette was very happy to be Goldilocks. "But who
will play the parts of Mama Bear and Papa Bear?" she asked.
"I'll be Mama Bear," said Greta.
"And I could be Papa Bear," suggested Raggedy Andy.

"But wait!" interrupted Babette. "We don't have any costumes."

Sunny Bunny knew just where to go for hats and scarves and lots of things.

"But we don't have a single piece of scenery," said Raggedy Andy, clapping his hand on his forehead.

"We'll use what we have, and the audience will just have to pretend," said Raggedy Ann.

   Bubbles the Clown, The Camel with the Wrinkled
Knees, and Tallyho the Wooden Horse sat patiently waiting
for the play to begin. They were very happy playing their
roles as members of the audience.

"Okay," said Raggedy Andy. "Everybody get to your places."

Raggedy Dog and Raggedy Cat were in charge of making the curtain open and close. Each took a corner and slowly opened the curtain.

"Once upon a time," began Raggedy Ann, "three bears lived in a cottage in the middle of the woods. There was a Papa Bear, a Mama Bear, and there was a Baby Bear. Right outside the woods lived a pretty little girl whose hair was so golden that everyone called her Goldilocks. One day, while the bears were away, Goldilocks decided to take a long walk through the woods."

Babette skipped onto the "stage."

"Oh!" she exclaimed. "What a lovely little cottage. I think I'll stop in and see if anyone is at home." And Babette pretended she was opening a door.

"My!" Babette exclaimed. "Look at these bowls full of porridge!"

"What bowls?" Tallyho whispered loudly.

"These bowls, silly," said Babette, pointing to nothing in front of her. And then Babette said the parts about "too hot," "too cold," and "just right."

"And then Goldilocks went into the bedroom," said
Raggedy Ann. And Babette tried all the beds, finally falling
sound asleep right on the floor.

"Very soon," Raggedy Ann continued, "the three bears came home."

Raggedy Andy, Greta, and Grouchy Bear ran onto the stage. Grouchy Bear bumped right into Babette.

For a moment, Babette forgot that she was acting in the play. "Watch where you're going!" she cried.

"Sunny Bunny is shining the light in my eyes," said Grouchy Bear. "I can't see anything."

"Sorry," called Sunny Bunny, as he lowered the flashlight.

Then the play went on.

"Who's been eating my porridge?" Raggedy Andy asked.

"Who's been sitting in my chair?" Greta asked.

"Never mind the porridge and the chairs," grumbled Grouchy Bear. "Why is Babette—I mean—that girl—sleeping in my bed?"

Everyone giggled.

"Goldilocks woke up and saw the bears standing beside her," Raggedy Ann continued.

Babette jumped up from the floor and ran from the stage as quickly as she could.

"They must have looked very ferocious," Raggedy Ann said with a laugh.

"And Goldilocks ran home and never came back to the cottage again. The end," Raggedy Ann said when the story was over.

"Hurray!" cried The Camel, and everyone started clapping—even Percy and Tim.

In fact, Percy and Tim were so busy clapping that they forgot to hold up the curtain.

Down it came, right on top of the actors as they were taking their bows.

Even Raggedy Ann couldn't help laughing at that!

"That was fun!" exclaimed Bubbles.

"Can we do another play?" asked Sunny Bunny.

"How about 'Sleeping Beauty'?" asked Babette. "I would like to play the part of Beauty!"

"How about '*Black* Beauty'?" suggested Tallyho.

"We can do lots of different stories," said Raggedy Ann. "The painters won't be through for at least a few days. But, for now, we had better put everything back the way we found it."

"Things haven't turned out so bad after all," said Raggedy Andy. "You said we should make the best of things," he said to Raggedy Ann, "and that's just what we did."

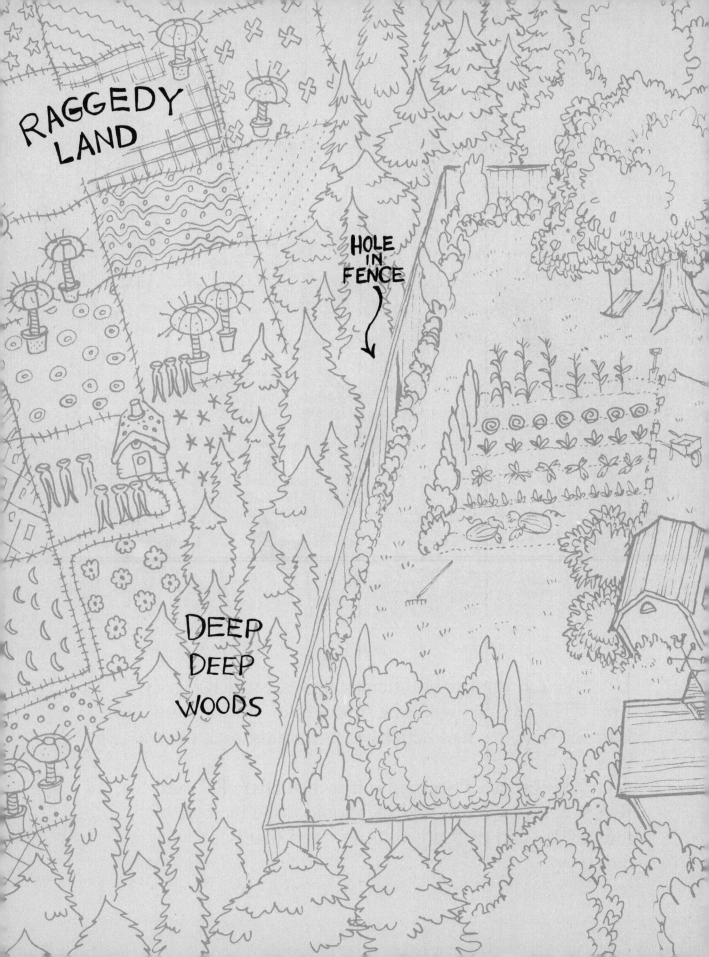